Book Crooks!

By J. J. Marlee

Illustrated by Francesco Legramandi

Batman created by Bob Kane with Bill Finger

A Random House PICTUREBACK® Book

Random House 🏠 New York

All rights reserved. Published in the United States by Random House Children's Books, a division of Penguin Random House LLC, 1745 Broadway, New York, NY 10019, and in Canada by Penguin Random House Canada Limited, Toronto. Pictureback, Random House, and the Random House colophon are registered trademarks of Penguin Random House LLC.

rhcbooks.com

ISBN 978-0-525-64739-3 (trade) — ISBN 978-0-525-64740-9 (ebook)

Printed in the United States of America   10 9 8 7 6 5 4 3 2 1

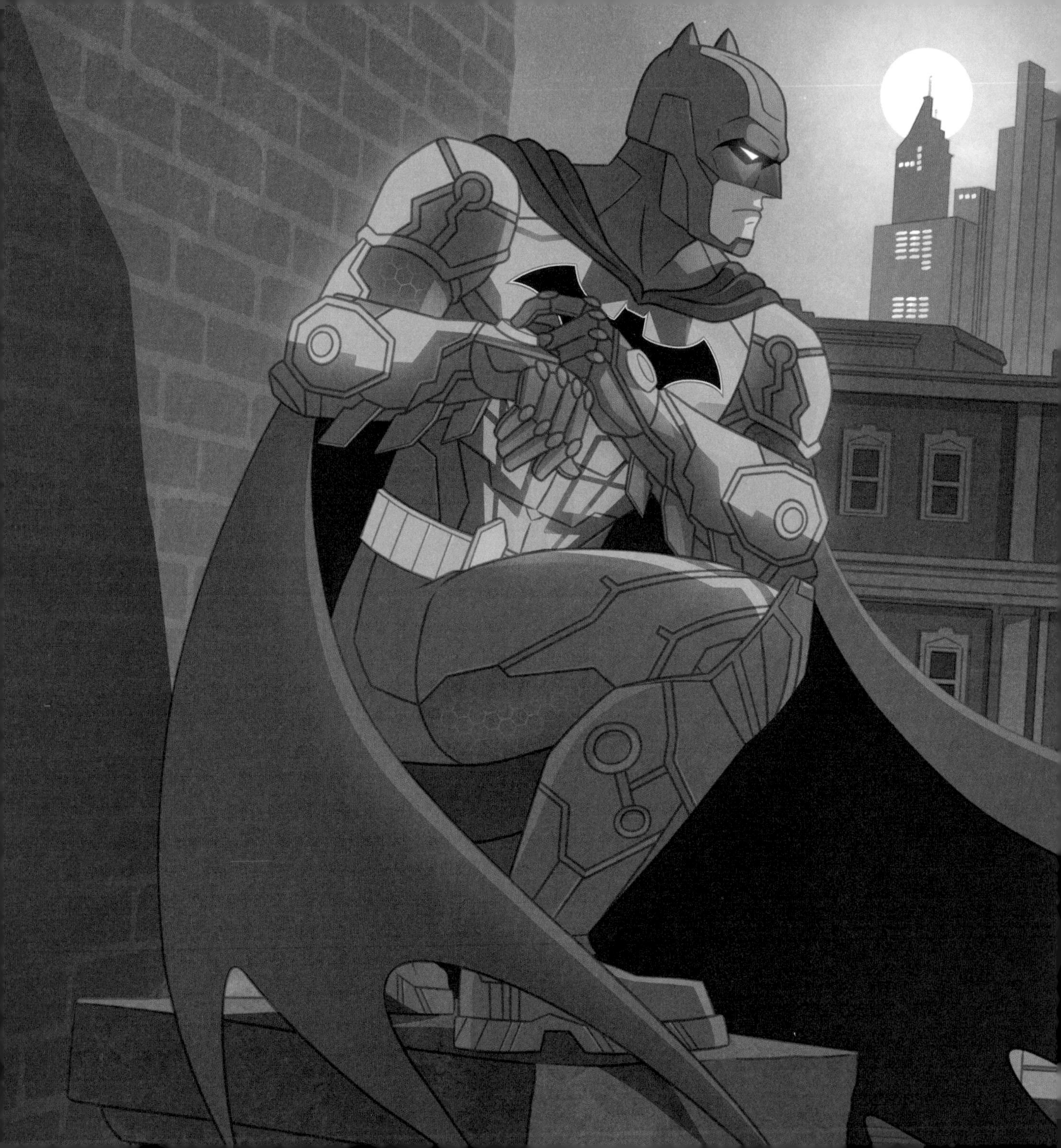

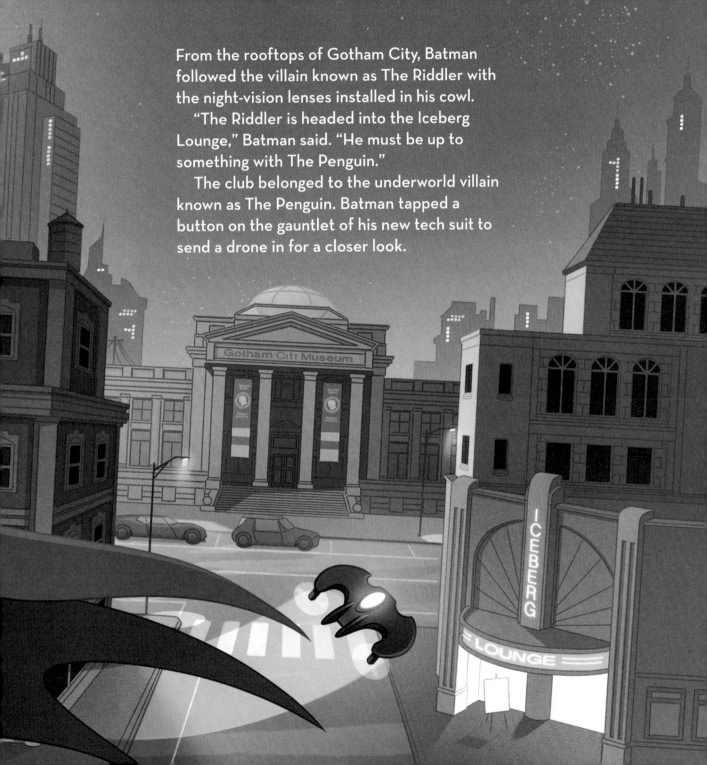

From the rooftops of Gotham City, Batman followed the villain known as The Riddler with the night-vision lenses installed in his cowl.

"The Riddler is headed into the Iceberg Lounge," Batman said. "He must be up to something with The Penguin."

The club belonged to the underworld villain known as The Penguin. Batman tapped a button on the gauntlet of his new tech suit to send a drone in for a closer look.

"A book with a jewel-encrusted cover and a gold case to keep it in!" The Penguin said. "It's priceless—and *I* want it!"

"Not only that, but the book contains riddles that haven't been read in two thousand years," The Riddler replied. "Now, *that* is what *I* call priceless!"

"It's a bargain for you," The Riddler went on, laughing out loud at the thought of all those delicious riddles. "You get the book to sell to the highest bidder. *I* get to read it. And we'll both have a good laugh."

"Deal," The Penguin replied.

"We'll see who has the last laugh," Batman said, listening in on the villains' plan with his drone. "I'd better get to the museum and catch them in the act."

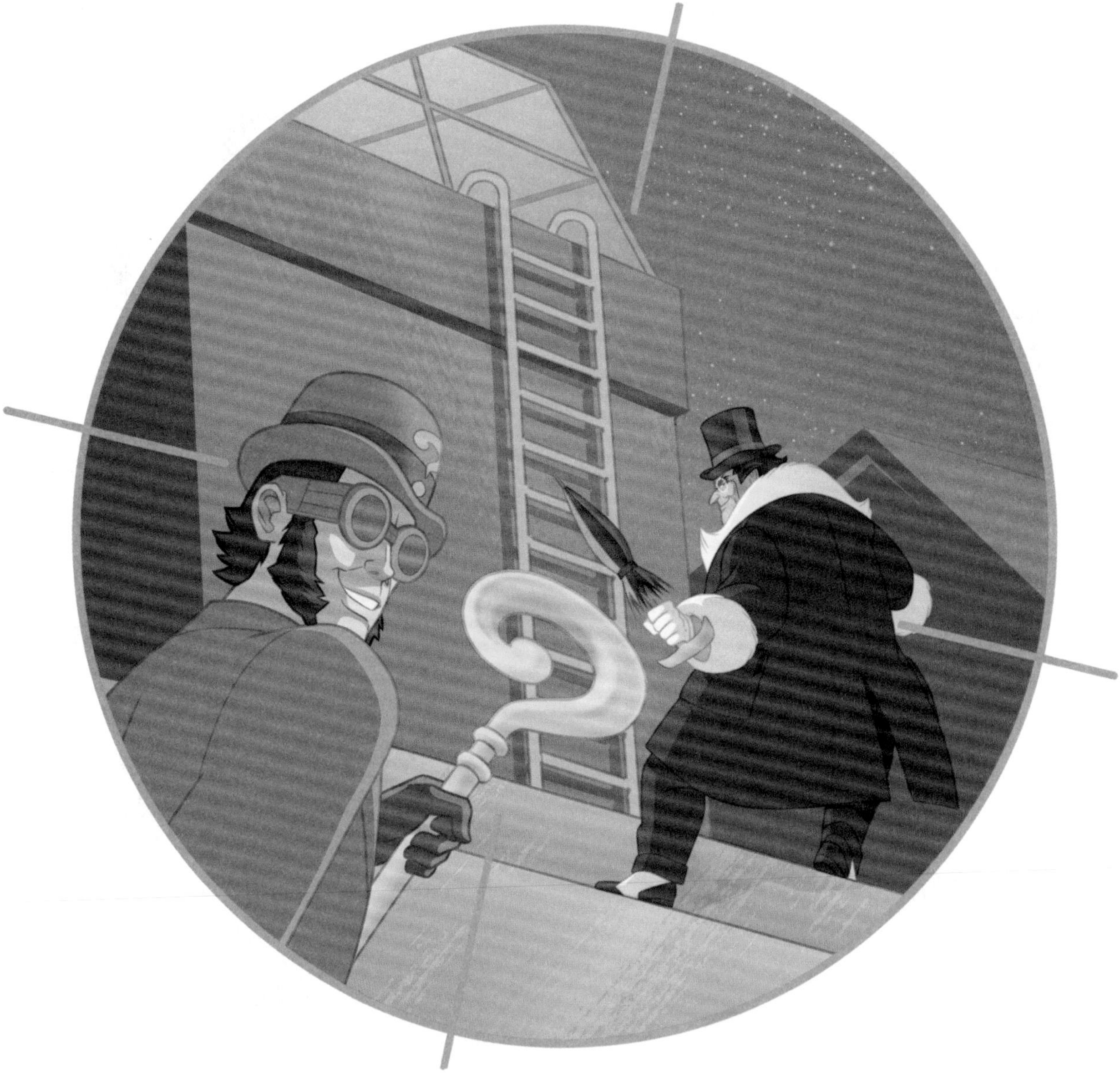

Racing over rooftops and swinging from his Batrope, the Caped Crusader quickly reached the Gotham City Museum. It was already dark and closed for the night when he slipped inside.

Inside, The Penguin and The Riddler had already gotten past the museum's security defenses and opened the glass case containing the book.

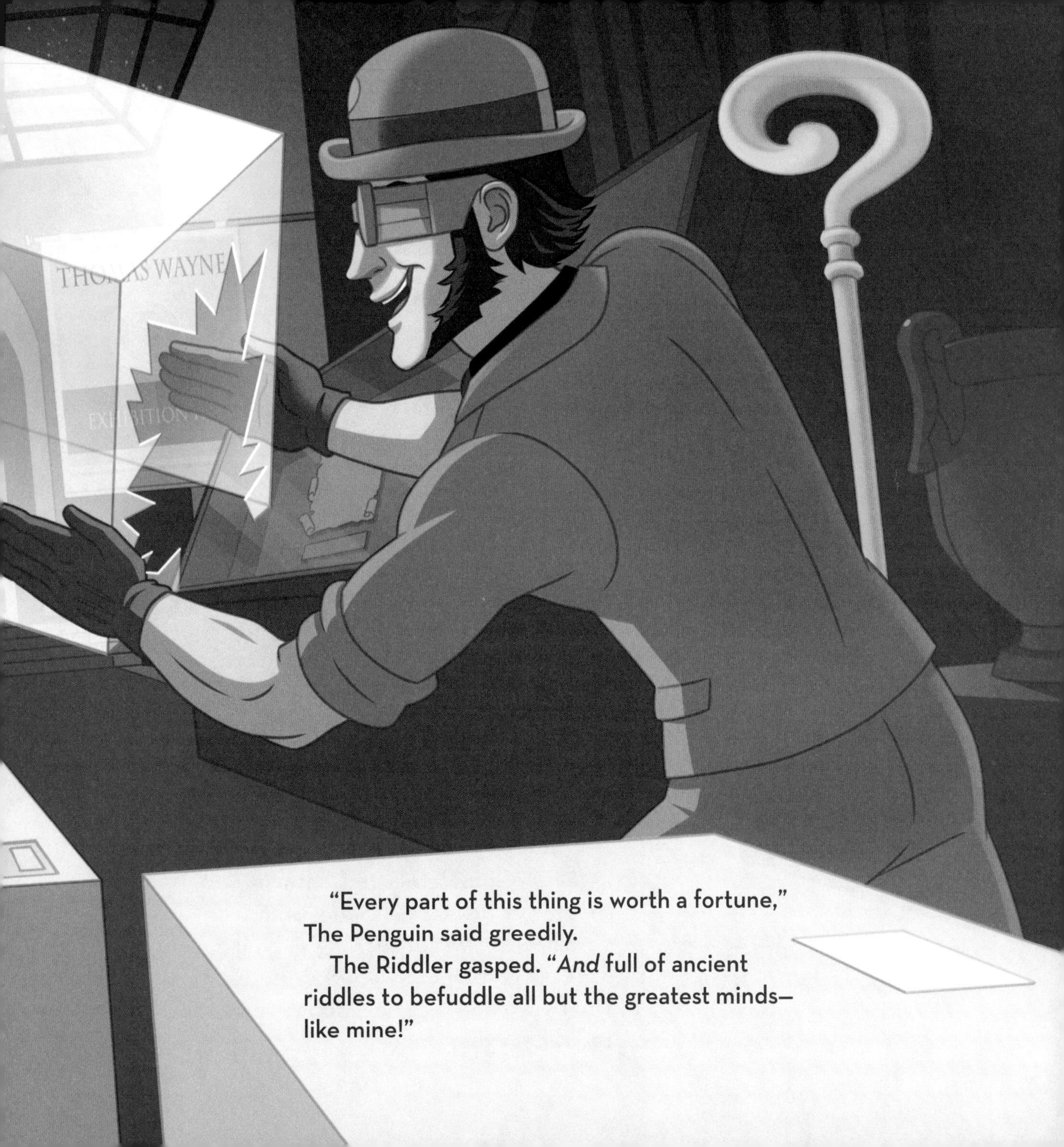

“Every part of this thing is worth a fortune,” The Penguin said greedily.

The Riddler gasped. “*And* full of ancient riddles to befuddle all but the greatest minds—like mine!”

"STOP RIGHT THERE!" Batman
shouted as he leapt into the room.
   "Since you've got such a great mind,
you take care of the Caped Crusader,"
The Penguin said as he grabbed the book
and ran for the window.

The Penguin clicked a button on his umbrella, causing rotary blades to spring out and start spinning. It was a helicopter!

"Sorry, gents, but I need to check out," he said as he headed toward a museum window.

Batman touched another button on his gauntlet. The drone that had been hovering outside crashed into The Penguin, sending him flying back into the room.

The Penguin slammed into a wall—*Oof!*—and the priceless book was launched into the air.

CRASH!

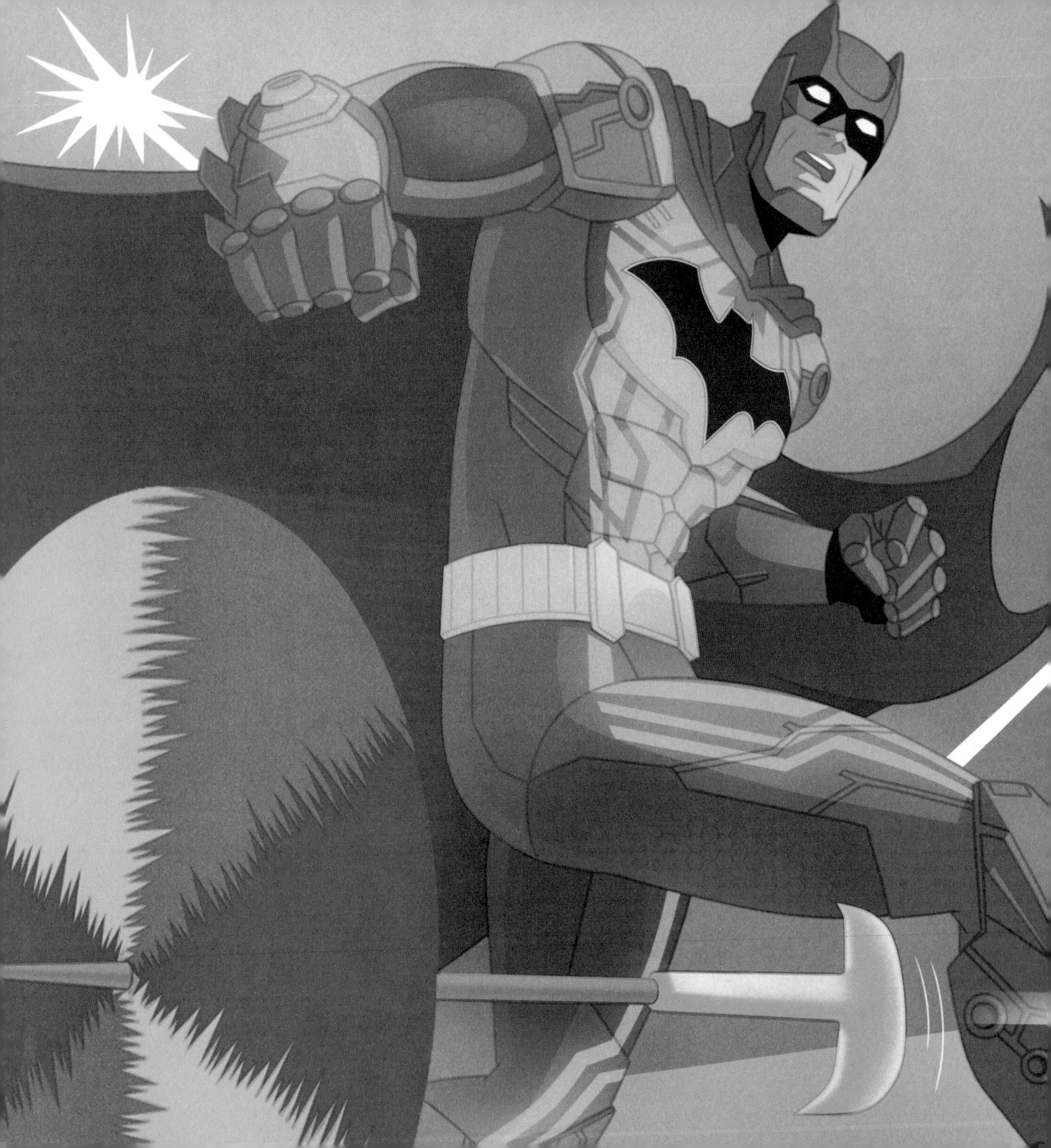

Taken by surprise, The Riddler laughed as the book fell into his hands! Meanwhile, the helicopter umbrella bounced around the room, blocking Batman from stopping him.

"I got the book! I got the book!" The Riddler giggled gleefully to himself as he ran down the hall. But he knew the propeller blades wouldn't stop Batman for long.

The Riddler was almost to the museum's front doors when Batman swooped down in front of him!

"It's not going to be that easy, Riddler," Batman said. "Hand over the book."

"You should always read with a good light," The Riddler said, activating his cane. Suddenly, there was a blinding flash! It made Batman stagger back for a moment.

FLASH

When Batman opened his eyes, he found himself facing not just one image of The Riddler, but *four* of them!

"Riddle me this, Batman—which Riddler is the real Riddler?" all The Riddlers asked in unison. "I knew this hologram projector would come in handy!"

But Batman wasn't so easily fooled. He flipped on his night vision, and in the hazy green glow, the holograms disappeared.

"The *right* Riddler is the one on the left!" Batman answered as he hurled a Batarang. The Riddler fell back, losing his grip on the cane and the priceless book.

When Commissioner Gordon arrived, The Penguin and The Riddler were already handcuffed on the museum steps.

"They're all yours," Batman said. "And I'll make sure the book gets back where it belongs."

"Good work, Batman," Commissioner Gordon said. The two villains scowled and grumbled as the policeman praised the hero. "Don't worry, you two. You'll have plenty of time to read in jail."

Inside the quiet museum, Batman carefully opened the book before putting it back. It took him a few moments to translate the first ancient riddle. He thought about it for a moment. Then when the World's Greatest Detective figured it out, he laughed and laughed.